PIPPA PLUM
TIME TRAVELLER

Pamela May Jones

ISBN 978-1-956696-23-3 (paperback)
ISBN 978-1-956696-24-0 (digital)

Rushmore Press LLC
1 800 460 9188
www.rushmorepress.com

Printed in the United States of America

PIPPA PLUM
TIME TRAVELLER

No.
1

Oᴎᴇ ᴅᴀʏ ᴀs Pɪᴘᴘᴀ Pʟᴜᴍ having left school was in her bedroom at her Mother's House which was called Lark's Flight because every Spring the Larks would be nesting in the nest boxes they had put onto their cottage. When Pippa's Mother and Father moved into the cottage they saw the lark's flying overhead which gave her Mother the Idea of calling the cottage Lark's Flight.

Anyway said Floss the fairy I am getting myself confused, now where was I.? Oh! Yes, Pippa Plum was in her bedroom at her Mother's Cottage, packing her belongings as she was going to move into her Little Cottage which was called Poppy Field Cottage because there was a field beside the cottage full of Poppies. She thought now she was thirty in human years it was time to have a place of her own. So she looked around Celrin and found this lovely little cottage beside a river and having the Poppy Field at the other side. There was a lovely little stone fireplace, with brass fender and dog irons. In front of that was a bright red rug, and she imagined there being a lovely, Black cat asleep on it. The people who had the cottage before her had gone to live in France so had left all the furniture which was really lovely, so Pippa Plum did not have to buy any.

There was a little black ebony settle by the side of the fire with embroidered cushions, and an embroidered, seat cushion which ran all the way along the, little settles seating area. Then there were four black ebony chairs and two carver chairs which also had embroidered cushions

There was the black ebony welsh dresser to put all her Plates and things on.

The ebony table was square but you could make it longer by putting two leaves one at each end. On it was a lovely lace cover and a Venetian, glass vase of red poppies.

With a little note, tie to them which said Welcome, to your new home Pippa. It was from one of the neighbours she had yet to meet.

She wondered around the kitchen the cupboards were painted bright red, it was rather cheery it made the whole kitchen look cosy. I know who made these cupboards said Pippa Plum, Richard, Celine and Catrin's dad. The kitchen had a welsh slate floor, which was shiny not dull it looked like someone had polished them. There was a big rug on some of the floor, brightly coloured with reds, green, blues, and yellows. The cooker was also painted red it was a big iron cooker with things that looked like hot plates

Then she went upstairs to see the two bedrooms, one was a huge room with a very big window to look at the views.

It had a big double bed in it in bright blue and the wardrobes and dressing table were blue also. Richard strikes again she laughed. The carpet on the floor was multi coloured to brighten up the room.

Then the little bedroom was done out in pink furniture, which had a single bed in it. The carpet was blue with little flowers on it in white. The little multi covered quilt off my bed will look lovely in here I will have to ask mam to make me a double one.

She flew back down the stairs and started to bring all her personal little things into the cottage. Then she put some fairy tea in her teapot with some water and some fairy dust and left it to brew. She got out some bread and cut a slice of it added some butter and some jam. Poured out her tea and took the snack into her sitting room sat down and began to eat it. Mmm. She thought this strawberry jam the jam fairy made is good I will have to get some more.

When she had finished she put her dishes into the sink and added some water and a sprinkle of fairy dust and left it to do its work. What does the fairy dust do children? Asked Floss the fairy.

The children came back with it washes it dries and it puts them away. Correct said Floss, you may each have a gold star. All the children laughed and said hurray. The doorbell rang, Post for Pippa Plum said the elf who came to the door. Hello Eric how are you today?

I'm fine thank you said the Elf. Can you sign for this please said Eric. It's come from America said Eric. Oh! I wonder who it can be from?, Said Pippa. Well open it and see said Eric. Mm. Pippa Plum said, well said Eric the Elf? Oh! It's from a Professor Fish he's from a University there. They want my help doing some research for them. Well, said Eric I must be off now. Bye. Mm Bye Eric, Pippa Plum said a little preoccupied with the letter.

Professor Fish said that he had found something quite

Unusual from and ancient tribe of Indians Could you time travel and look into it? Please. Oh! Yippee an assignment at last.

She dashed upstairs in her excitement she forgot to fly, and started to pack a suitcase, shorts, trousers, skirts, tops, shirts, undies, towels, toothbrush, toothpaste, comb, brush, soap, fairy dust. Think that will be enough said Pippa Plum. Then she got out her special coat that was waterproof, rainproof snow proof, sand proof in fact it was practically indestructible. She then called for her little pony sunbeam with her special fairy whistle. Sunbeam came flying up turning a summersault in the process.

Right, Sunbeam we have to go to America. We need to get your saddle, bridle, saddlebags etc., and then I will stand us in a big square I have marked out and throw up the fairy dust, which should take us to America when I have spoken the secret words. Xjgfnhkdfhyebnvl, gijkeg skuihj America. No, one but Pippa Plum knew those words even the secret society she belonged too, as they all had their own secret words.

Now, all of a sudden, there was a great big rush of wind, which whirled around them like a big typhoon which sucked them both up and next thing they know they are in America, right outside the University of Idaho city She tied Sunbeam up outside the University on a special rail they had for tying horses too, and then went inside the University to find the Professor. Is Professor Fish Available?

Please? Pippa said. Who might say is asking said a snooty receptionist? I am Pippa Plum the Time Traveller said Pippa He wrote to me and asked me to come. Thank you said the snooty receptionist. I will inform the Professor you are here. Would you like to take a seat? Thank you said Pippa Plum and sat down.

The snooty receptionist picked up the phone and dialled a number. Oh! Hello Professor I have a Pippa Plum here to see you said the snooty receptionist.

The reply from the Professor was Will you escort her to my room please Amelia.

Yes of course Professor Fish.

Miss Plum would you care to follow me.

Thank you said Pippa Plum and followed who she now knew was called Amelia to go to Professor Fish's room at the University.

Welcome, Pippa said the Professor, please be seated.

Thank you said Pippa, how may I be of help to you? She said. Well we have found this object that belongs to an Ancient Indian tribe called the Glummpopo. It is almost dated to the year 0098. What is the object asked Pippa Plum? It's a ceremonial knife of the Chief of the Glummpopo. May I look said Pippa Plum? Of course you may said the Professor. Pippa picked it up wow its is

Beautiful Look at all the diamonds, rubies, emeralds and what is the design do you think said the professor? It's symbolic for a ritual called kcnfkfbw bfkev. Oh! Said the Professor, I have never heard of that. No, you wouldn't I only know as I am a member of this secret society and we all pass on facts we learn about anything.

Well, Professor what do you want me to do? I would like to go back to 0098 with you and find the Lost Tribe of the Glummpopo. Right will tomorrow be soon enough. Fine said the Professor. Tomorrow it is. What time he asked Pippa? Oh! Around nine a.m. should be soon enough she said. Now I will show you to your quarters, I have made arrangements for you to stay at the University, hope that is alright? The Professor said. Fine said Pippa I might need to read up on the Glummpopo. Well we have an extensive library here for you to do just that.

Where is your horse Sunbeam I believe you called her?

The Professor said. She's just outside said Pippa. Well, we will take her to the stables on the way to your room on Campus. The Professor said. Lovely, Pippa said and smiled.

They untied Sunbeam and took her to the stables.

Then they carried on with the saddlebags which held Pippa's clothes to her room on Campus.

Right Pippa, I will leave you to unpack and take a shower etc., If we meet around seven in the front office where you came in. Great said Pippa, see you at seven.

Pippa unpacked her meagre belongings and placed them in the closet that's what the Americans call a wardrobe

Said Floss the fairy to the fairy children who were sitting so engrossed in the story that they forgot it was playtime.

Shall I carry on said Floss or do you want to go and play.

Story, story, story chanted the children.

Pippa got undressed and went to take a shower in the

What children? Bathroom they laughed.

Then she dries herself off and puts on her clean clothes.

I think I will have a lie down its only six thirty. She nodded off to sleep to be awoken by her alarm clock that she had set before going for her nap. Six fifty five right must fly. She got her purse(bag) that's what the Americans call it and flew down the stairs and across the Campus to meet the Professor, dead on seven. Just made it she laughs. Well the restaurant is just around the corner to the Campus do you want to fly or shall I drive my special car. No I can fly that far said Pippa.

So he walked and she flew to the little Italian restaurant, to have dinner. They had Tuna Italian with a little Lime Juice Cordial instead of wine, as fairies get quite tipsy on wine.

Now about tomorrow said Pippa, you do have all the right equipment, don't you? I had a friend of mine send you the special coat you will need. Yes, I received it yesterday, said the Professor. Good Pippa Said. You will have need of that. Why is it so special asked the Professor? Well, it will stand anything from rain, to snow; to sand blizzards in fact it is made from a special material only the fairies know how to make. No-but-the-fairy world know it exists so you must not tell a living soul. Promise said Pippa. Yes, I promise said the Professor. Now enjoy you Tuna Italian.

So they sat and talked, and talked until it was time to go

To get some sleep. Good night Pippa, Good night Professor call me Andrew said the Professor see you around nine.

She snuggled down in her bed after her usual night time business of getting washed etc., and was soon fast asleep. She slept until her fairy alarm clock went off at eight thirty were by she arose and got showered and dressed and was down by the front desk at nine.

Hello Professor said Pippa, hello Pippa said Andrew.

We will take my special car to where we want to go

Said Andrew, I have made all the arrangements like you said They drove off the Campus in the car and when out of sight it turned into guess what children? Asked Floss a flying car said the children. No, said Floss a helicopter and they laughed.

Well they were by now out in the dessert where Andrew(Professor) had made a huge stone circle, sorry had to use the stones everything else would blow away.

That's alright said Pippa as long as it's a circle. Should we take the car, no said Pippa it might confuse them.

She placed quite a lot of fairy dust just inside the stone circle Said a few magic words. Oxklsnrjkvnrejdbfjocdee3 0098 and she and Andrew stood in the middle and then it began, the wind blew, then whistled, then whirled

Until it became a typhoon and drew them up into the air

And plonked them down just as they had stood in the stone circle

Wow, Andrew said that was some trip. Yes, it is quite exhilarating isn't it said Pippa Plum. I get a kick every time I go time travelling. How often do you go time travelling? Asked Andrew, Oh! Quite a few times over, the last few years. Said Pippa Do you often take people with you asked Andrew I try not too said Pippa, they can cause all sorts of problems if they mess about and change history someone might not get born or someone could die before his or her time. Oh! Said Andrew I did not realize things like that could happen, Oh! Yes you have to be very careful. Well what do we do now asked Andrew? Well, we scout around and look for any signs of the Glummpopo Oh! I see some sign of a moccasin foot. Said Pippa where said Andrew? Here look someone is walking that way and then they disappear. How odd, where have they gone? I don't know said Andrew it is very strange indeed. Oh! Look footprints again, and then they disappear again. This is very, very strange. So they kept following the footprints each time they'd disappeared to reappear somewhere else. This went on for about, Twenty fairy miles(I don't know in human miles Floss said.) but it will be rather a lot.

Then all of a sudden, something whizzed past them with wrrrrrrr, wrrrrrrr, what on earth was that asked Pippa? I don't know said Andew. They looked around and there was

This little flying man about two foot tall, he'd flown past them so quickly they only heard his wings. Wow, said Pippa Plum it's the first time I've ever seen a white Pigmy.

Then this little voice came from below them, who are you and what are you doing on Glummpopo land, Oh! said Pippa are you the Lost Tribe of Glummpopo, we are not lost said the little man, we've live here for centuries.

How can, this be, said Pippa Plum its only 0098 now?. Well, we have a different counting system than you,

Perhaps, that's why. Oh! Yes, I see said Pippa Plum.

Could we meet your people asked Pippa and Andrew? Yes, said the Glummpopo man. Now children this is why the Glummpopo man can speak our language, they have a Special Power, so they can, speak, to anyone. Floss said.

So the Chief of the Glummpopo took them to his village, to meet his family and the other villagers. Everyone cried

Nftrhsrpz, Wpirq,-Ounbvnashv, which means hello in

Glummpopo the Chief spoke to his people in their

Own language but I will translate to you said the Chief

They say welcome, come sit and eat with us, sing with us and pray with us. Please sit.

So Andrew (Professor) and Pippa Plum sat and ate with the Lost Tribe of Glummpopo. Then the Glummpopo danced for them, and sang for them. Introduced everyone

Said we will show you our Hidden City tomorrow and then showed them to a hunt to have a sleep.

Well, morning came and the Glummpopo started shouting

Pjfagjejejbliy, they have seen something which should not be here cries the Chief. Come Look. So they went with the Chief. Then they saw it, it was a tremendous size,

Big Oval shape with great big green eyes, I thought they did not exist said Andrew, I have never doubted that they existed said Pippa, yes but space men, well, why not said Pippa. They watched as the door swung down onto the Glummpopo lands earth which was sort of half sand and half earth. Then there appeared a huge Man as tall as a House all dressed in silver. Who held up his hands and spoke. We come in peace said this voice, we do not wish to harm you. We are time travellers from the plant earth two.

Pippa Plum could not believe her ears, from earth? How can they be so tall? Pippa had not heard the two part of his message. They are Giants said Andrew not from our earth but earth two. Where ever that is? Well, let's ask him said Pippa Plum. Hello, Sir, Where is your plant earth two?

It is a million, trillion light years away he said We come in peace, yes, I heard that said Pippa Plum time traveller

We are time travellers too, we come from earth one.

How can we assist you said Andrew(Proffessor)? We just want to find out about plants, water, sand, animal life,

Insect's, things of interest. We won't take anything without asking and my name is Zarron. I come with friends Zuccon, and Zeddon. They are unusual names said Pippa Plum, yes, we are working through our Alphabet said Zarron. That's funny we have an alphabet too said Pippa Plum. ABCDEFGHIJKLMNOPQRSTUVWXYZ funny said Zarron it's like ours but ours is the other way round.

Perhaps, our world is the mirror image of yours said Zarron.

If I may ask do all earths people have wings? Zarron asked?.

No said Pippa I am a fairy I come from a secret world on earth only the Very Old and the very young can see us.

That is funny said Zarron we have <u>a secret fairy</u> world too but ours live above us, we are the ones that live below.

It is almost like a mirrored world to ours said Pippa Plum, well I must go now said Pippa I must seek the Hidden City of Glummpopo.

What is the Hidden City of Glummpopo Zarron asked?.

Well, on earth we have legends which tell of Lost Cities, Lost Mines, Camelot and King Arthur, various other myths. People like the time travellers try to seek them. I am here to find the Lost and Hidden City of Glummpopo. We came upon a jewel encrusted knife and carbon dated it to the year 0098. That is interesting said Zarron. May I contact you about that sometimes? Yes, of course said Pippa Plum.

Where is the Chief Andrew? He's ready to show us the Hidden City of Glummpopo. They walked up to the Chief and they set off for the Hidden City. Many miles they walked, Pippa was lucky she could fly when she got tired.

Then they came upon well, of all things to find here.

Guess what they found children? A House, No, but a Pyramid. A Pyramid said the fairy children. Yes a gigantic Pyramid, but you could not see it from above as there was a Special Shield of Light Protecting it. OH!.......The children said.

They walked up to the Pyramid and the Chief of the Glummpopo (which was as it turned out a white race of Pygmy's.) spoke these magic words jbwmngqpyIrewg#pohj

Phhk. Oh!..............the fairy children said.

Suddenly, they heard a great big sound like stone being rubbed on stone, and a door suddenly appeared in the Pyramid. Everyone stepped forward to see. but all they could see were some stone steps leading down, down, down. Goodness Pippa said, I'm glad I can fly at least I won't have to walk down that lot. Well, Andrew said it's not the walking down it's the climbing up that will be the problem.

Well, it took ages before everyone was down the steps and into a great chamber. Pippa Plum of course was the first one there being she flew. She was flying around looking at the Hieroglyphic's, that were painted on the wall Wow, these are brilliant she said They tell of the Lost Tribe of the Glummpopo and how the hidden city was built so that they could be protected from invaders who had been threatening them.

The invaders were from another planet and they came in the year 0096. With swords of light which breathed fire one minute and black liquid the next, but could cut of your arms or legs without touching them.

They poured the black liquid over everything and then breathed the fire onto it destroying everything and anybody who got in their way

They took children from their Mother's and if anyone got in the way they just killed them.

They were only about five feet tall with long brown hair tied up in a big knot on top of their heads waving about like a tail but at the ends of the hairs it was like little lights coming from the ends which sizzled when they touched anything. They breathed smoke from their nostrils and their eyes where blood red the entire eye. Not like ours which had whites and then blue, brown, or green

Said Floss the fairy. Ugh! The fairy children did not like that at all.

Well, the fighting went on, and on, and on until most of the Tribe of Glummpopo, that had not been able to escape, to the safety of the Pyramid were killed. Then the invaders started digging up the earth in a certain spot and found some sort of crystal rock formation and quarried it until they had it all. Then they just got in their space ship (is what we'll call it) said Floss the Fairy. Flew away with a big HHHHHHHHick-up ype sound

When the Glummpopo sensed that the invaders had gone because they had something in their special powers that told them this. They came out to bury their dead Well, actually they did not bury them said Floss the fairy. They made a special alter and placed them on it and then with some sort of power were everyone joined hands, they just vanished into thin air. One minute there the next gone.

They then gave up a mighty cry mumbala, mumbala

They chanted over and over again, Mumbala, mumbala. The Little Lost Tribe of the Glummpopo, moarned, their dead Then all of a sudden it changed and became laughter, flying down from the sky came all the Glummpopo that had died, how on earth said Pippa Plum?

They cannot die they are invincible, they die and then they are set upon the alter, and they are sent to the place were, well, it's like a place or palace in the sky and suddenly, they arise and fall down to earth. Alive as if by a miracle, Mumbala, is a GOD to them. He lives in the palace in the sky

Wow, Pippa Plum said. Wow, Can we see the palace in the sky.

No, Only the Lost Tribe of Glummpopo can see him and his palace, Said the Chief of the Glummpopo.

Well, now the Little Chief spoke some more magic words and then a door slide down and allowed them to enter this other chamber. Inside was so much gold, that they could not imagine where it came from. There were statues, coins, swords, crowns, almost everything you can imagine but made in gold. Pippa Plum said to the Chief of the Glummpopo Where does all this come from. He answered

With a smile Glummpopo has gold, silver, copper, and any other precious metal man wants. Even some he has not heard of before, but as it is hidden from them unless they find the secret of the Pyramid, it is safe. For only a few know of its existence, all my people and you two.

He then took us to another part of the pyramid and spoke a few magic words. nvrehjypojok, and another door slide across to show us its treasures only this time it was diamonds, emeralds, rubies, sapphires, and white, pink and black pearls. Oh! My Goodness Andrew exclaimed. And mine too said Pippa Plum.

Yes, this is the Lost Treasure of Glummpopo, it was all stolen once but we got out our Magic Purple Powder and time travelled to recover it They will not be able to steal it again as we have put booby traps you call them all over the place. We turned them off because we were going to show you the Treasures. We used Magic Purple Powder

To get here Pippa Plum said.

Yes, the Chief said, you are one of the fairy peoples, who know of such things, only secrets The Fairies know.

The Chief said.

The Chief went into the jewel room and picked up a string of black pearls, which he gave to Pippa Plum. Oh! Chief are these really for me. Yes, said the chief, special fairies get special pearls. He gave Andrew a diamond as big as an eye. Andrew thanked him and shook his hand.

Andrew said now, Chief I have something for you, he got his rucksack and took out the ceremonial knife, which he gave to the Chief, where did you get this said the Chief

It was found at the bottom of the sea by a Treasure Hunter, how it got there we do not know. Now I have returned it to its people, my job is done thanks to Pippa Plum the time traveller.

One last secret to unfold The Chief said He open yet another door with no magic words. There in all its glory was the most stupendous waterfall. It was outside the Pyramid but you could not see it because of the Shield

Protecting both it and the Rain forest it protected which is were the Chief and all of his Tribe got there food, the animals and birds were protected by the Magic Shield of Glummpopo which was set upon a rock right in the middle of the rainforest, no one knows what metal it is made from, or where it came from, or were the Lost Tribe of Glummpopo came from the Little race of White Pygmy's

Looking after and protecting this wonderful little world of Glummpopo.

PIPPA PLUM TIME TRAVELLER

No. 2

ARLY ONE AFTERNOON, PIPPA PLUM received a knock on the door,

She flew to answer it, hello said a voice, she looked about but could see no one, so she went to close the door, don't do that said the voice, where are you? Pippa asked. Down here said the voice, Pippa looked down to see what she thought was a little girl, but it wasn't a little girl, she was a white pygmy from the Glummpopo Tribe, they were supposed to be lost, but Pippa found them on her last time travel journey. Hello said the little pygmy girl, my name Marta Umbopo; she was dressed in a grass skirt and colourful top, with a garland of flowers around her neck a bit like the Hawaiian women of Hawaii. I have come to ask if you could help us find the healing mask of Glummpopo. It is made of green jade, and about, the size of your face. Marta Umbopo said. Goodness Pippa said it must be worth a lot of money. Yes, Marta Umbopo said it is priceless for the eyes are diamonds the mouth is made of rubies and the nose is a very rare pink pearl. Will you help the Glummpopo to find it? Yes, Pippa, said. Who stole it? Well said Marta Umbopo we are not quite sure, but we heard that a Treasure Hunter had been searching for the Lost Tribe of Glummpopo and the Jade Healing Mask. Well, I never, it sounds like Douglas MacDougall he is a very determined man, I expect he has it.

Why is it so necessary for you to get it back?

Well, Marta said for one there is a map, on the back telling were our treasure stores are, and how to get there and secondly the Chief is very, very ill and the mask would heal him, he cannot die but we do not want to have to kill him to get him reborn again. The Mask would stop that. Right, when did you last see the Mask? The before yesterday Marta said. We had used it on the Chief, but he needs it still, so we went to fetch it and it was gone. Take me to where the Mask was.

Pippa Plum said. So Marta took hold of Pippa's hand and was just about to throw the green fairy dust when Pippa said Wait! I need to take a few things with me first. So she flew into her bedroom got her rucksack, threw a few clothes, toiletry's etc., and put the back on her back, now how do you imagine she could get her wings through a backpack said Floss, she had one designed to go round her wings, laughed some of the children.

Marta said are you ready Pippa and got hold of Pippa's hand and flew through the window. Made a circle of the green powder and said the magic words wjgehghbjeh then stood quite still, still holding Pippa's hand. Suddenly, the green fairy dust seemed to glow and then a cloud of green smoke and with a Whoshhhhhh the wind came, then became stronger and stronger until it was swirling, around like a typhoon, sucking them up, up, up, until they were somewhere in the middle.

Then just as suddenly, the wind stopped and they were in Glummpopo, right next to the Pyramid.

Marta spoke a few magic words ogjednkivob mfwpojwvojwsj and a door in the Pyramid slide open, to show Pippa yet another site she had not seen, a whole assortment of Masks all different and all made of something valuable, there was one mask she really liked and that was the crystal mask, it was decorated with blue sapphires for the eyes, rubies for the mouth and pearl for the nose, but it also had like a head band decorated in all different coloured jewels, and there was this fabulous thing to put round your neck, it sort of went into a pyramid shape but in reverse and then onto a long piece that went around your throat, all fabulous stones in a pattern of colour, a bit like a mosaic, but she did not recognise the design. Then with that went like a wide cuff type bangle all in the same stones as the necklace.

There was a beautiful golden mask, made of solid gold decorated with diamonds. Another one in solid silver decorated with rubies, another had emeralds, sapphires, nearly every valuable stone you could imagine. Then on a big block of stone which had been polished, there were just piles of jewels all set out in different colours. Another block had white, pink, black pearls in piles.

This is where the Jade Mask was stolen from, Pippa looked at the jade that would have surrounded the Jade Mask it was beautiful all intricately carved. There were ankle bracelets, bracelets, necklaces, earrings.

Pippa Plum looked around Douglas McDougall always left a sign when he had taken things. So she was looking for Ah! Yes! It was Douglas McDougall who had taken the mask, see here like a little snake all coiled up and ready strike, that's his mark alright.

Pippa thought now where would Douglas McDougall take the Jade Mask and who wanted it so badly. Mm. Let me think, Pippa Plum said, Tavish Mac Tavish, or Gwyn Jones are the real specialists, in stolen antiquities. I bet my last dollar it's one or the other, of them

Who's after the Jade Healing Mask, they will have a person who wants to buy it for some reason and who does not mind what it costs. Pippa said. A lot of the collectors have a secret room where they put them on display but no one sees them but themselves.

You mean that they just sit and admire them, yes, that's all they do, sit and admire them. Marta said. Yes, Pippa said. I can't see the fun in that Marta said. No, neither can I Pippa said.

Well, that's that Marta said, we know who took it, but not the reason why, where does that leave us then said Marta. In a boat without a paddle Pippa said laughing.

Now, why would he want a healing mask? Thought Pippa, she looked very puzzled. Perhaps, someone he knows is ill, Marta said. Perhaps but as to who it is or why he wants it. I do not know. All I know is that it's not his to just take; it belongs to the Glummpopo

Tribe. A tribe of white pygmy, only two feet tall, but who can fly, farther, than any fairy, can fly for they had wings on their feet as well as their normal wings.

They also could not die, if it seemed that they were dead, then they were put upon an alter and suddenly, they would disappear up into the sky, they spoke magic words and chanted things. Then a good cheer would go up, and they would all appear and be living again.

Then they had a huge celebration, to welcome them back into the fold of the tribe.

The tribe would sing and dance, dance and sing, sing and dance until everyone joined in the dance and they were twisting one way and then twisting the other almost like the conga. Everyone had a good time dancing and singing.

The river here is quite wide said Pippa, we will have to go further down the riverbank and see if we can cross there. Pippa said.

No, said Marta, we can use the canoe to go further downstream, so they climbed into a canoe, and paddled downstream until they came to a narrow part where they left the canoe and walked on stepping stones until they got across the river. Right where would Douglas MacDougall have gone to from here said Pippa? Well, the only way is to go through Umboto Land, but it would be a very dangerous trail for him if he did not know the way. Why? Pippa asked. Well, there are nasty insects which can bite you and in a matter of minutes you wouldn't be able to walk for at least twelve hours and that could mean you could be a meal for someone or something nasty. Marta said.

Then there is the swamp where crocodiles live, you have to cross that. Then you might fall into the quicksand and without help you could be stuck there. Then you have to pass through the Gorillas of Matumbi's land. Gorillas are not an animal to play with they can be very dangerous if roused or interfered with. Then last of all there is the jungle maze made by the Natouri tribe. Get lost in that and you're never seen again.

If that's the case what about us? Pippa asked. Well, I have been here before, so the only problem for us is the maze, I have never done it. Marta said. Well, Pippa said we can worry about that after, let's get going.

They came across a Skull on a pole with a number of other skulls dangling from it, this is Umboto Land'

It's a good job you have got your suit and boots on; the insects will have a problem with you, especially if, you put your guard down over your face. Marta laughed as she said it. Pippa asked well I'm not worried but what about you? I will be o.k. our tribe are immune to them something in the past when one of our ancestors got bitten, it did not seem to bother him after two hours. So as he had children they became immune. So then that's how it came to be with me, I was bitten but nothing happened except I had a big bump for a couple of hours.

Look there is one on your trousers, Pippa bashed it with the stick she was carrying and it fell to the ground. They walked on and on until they came to a swamp in which the crocodiles lived, they can be nasty if you're not careful said Marta, just keep close to me, and you should be o.k. I think that bright suit of yours will mesmerize them Marta laughed. Well, said Pippa it's a good suit because if it's warm you don't get too hot and if it's cold it keeps you warm, It keeps insects out with its special material which has insect repellent on it. Snakes cannot get you because they cannot find an opening to slither into or bite it's too thick. So far I've been kept safe with it. Suddenly, the Crocodiles started to slide into the water, just below where they wanted to go. So Marta skirted around them and went further downstream from where they were. Then all of a sudden splash they saw the crocodile turning, and spinning, spinning and turning, what is it they have Pippa asked?

Oh! It's a little deer from the size of it. Marta said. Oh! No, It's Mother is looking for it Pippa said, listen she's calling to it. Well, she's too late said Marta. Its gone forever those two have just ripped it apart.

Poor thing Pippa said, well, said Marta that's the way it goes out here. The Strongest survives the weakest dies.

Let's have a rest here said Marta; I need a drink and something to eat. Pippa searched in her pockets and handed Marta something wrapped in paper, what's this she asked? It's what is known as a snack bar. It gives you energy and keeps you going. Mm. Marta said it's very good. Then they had a drink of some water from the canteen it had some fairy dust added to it, so it would keep fresh and sweet tasting. Pippa said ready let's be off, then and started walking towards the quicksand, STOP Marta shouted. Pippa stopped leg in the air, do not put your foot down there, or you're a goner. Pippa did a turn mid- air lucky I used to be a ballet dancer Pippa said. Laughing as she thought goodness that was too close for comfort. Marta said let me go in front of you and make a trail for you to follow, Marta being a fairy could tread lightly to check if it was quicksand or not. If it was she left no print if it was alright she left her footprint in the sandy stuff. Pippa followed very carefully, she thought Oh! What I'd give to have my wings free at this moment. I must get my fashion designer to make me a suit I can have my wings free.

That's the quicksand gone through said Marta. Let's make a camp here for tonight and then we will be fresh in the morning. Fine by me Pippa said. She took off her helmet and placed it on a branch high enough to keep the creepy crawlies out with the face mask closed. She started to collect some branches from around and about the camp site, where she could keep an eye on things while Marta, got the food going, this back pack of yours is very good said Marta would you bring me one next time you come here. Oh! Pippa said you can have that one if you like I can always get another one for myself. Many thanks said Marta. She had lit the fire and got the pot out of the bag and some of the food Pippa had brought and was cooking over the fire. This wooden stick is very useful said Marta what is it. Oh! That little thing well, said Pippa it's called a wooden spoon and you use it for stirring things when you're either cooking or baking. You may have that too when we have finished with it. What do you normally stir you're food with? Oh! Just some old stick or whatever is handy.

Marta said. Foods ready when you are. Good I'm famished. Pippa Said.

She took the bowl from Marta; Mm. Boy does that smell good. Oh! Yes just what I needed said Pippa. Yes, it is good said Marta, want some more? No thank you Pippa said.

Good I'll do the washing up Pippa said laughing, how you have the nerve to say that you will do the washing up said Marta handing her the fairy dust and laughing. Pippa took it down to the river sprinkled some on the dishes and dipped them in the water, she dropped one as she was startled by something looking at her across the river. The dish flew up in the air and went back towards the camp fire. Marta caught it just as it got to the backpack. Good catch said Pippa, here catch the other.

Marta caught it and placed it in the backpack along with all the other things she had used. Pippa Unzipped her suit trousers and made her a sleeping bag. She had brought one for Marta in the backpack, but she never needed one as her trousers were designed to be made into one. You're Fashion designer is very clever, I would never have thought of that idea. Marta said.

Yes, she is brilliant; I want her to make something I can get my wings free in next, that swamp would not have been a problem then. Pippa said. Yes, wings are very useful sometimes.

Good night Marta said after throwing more wood on the fire. They settled down to sleep, only to be awoken by the little birds singing in the morning.

Pippa said I will make the breakfast, you go and have you're wash. Fine thanks said Marta. As she took her towel and soap down to the river. Suddenly, something very strange happened, fish were jumping out of the water, that's strange thought Marta there are no crocodiles about, why are the fish behaving like this? Then she remembered Pippa had used purple fairy dust to wash the dishes, could the fairy dust have affected the fish. She raced back to the camp to tell Pippa. Guess what! She said there are fish jumping out of the water where you washed the dishes with fairy dust, could it have affected them? Oh! Dear thought Pippa I never thought of that, when I washed the dishes. She said this to Marta, I suppose it could have affected them, it should not hurt them though. Well, anyone wanting fish now they would be easy to catch, do you want some for dinner. Marta said Laughing as she walked away back down to the river to wash. She washed herself and dried herself and then caught two fish for dinner in the towel. Whistling as she walked back to camp. There you are then, she said, dinner. Thanks Pippa said.

They packed up the camp, put out the fire with some sand and wandered around tidying up; they thought they would not use fairy dust in case of problems.

Right I'm done said Pippa, me too said Marta. Let's get going then. So they started off towards the Matumbi's Land, Gorillas are dangerous so be very, very careful. Yes, Pippa said.

Now, quietly said Marta, they did not say a word as they crossed in front of the big gorillas almost on their knees so as not to antagonise the Big Gorillas. Pippa being dressed in bright pink it was a wonder they were not attacked. They got past two of them and could walk upright again, until they came across another Gorilla eating, they got down low and crept along until they got behind him, we would not have had this trouble if we could use our wings Marta said, but you can. It's me that can't do it. I could not leave you here on your own could I, and if it was the other way around you wouldn't leave me. Marta said. Well, No I suppose not Pippa said.

Then they were through the territory of the Gorilla's and they could walk upright again, Wow! That was a bit scary said Pippa, Yes, Marta said, I was nervous about that. How much farther have we to go to get to where Douglas MacDougall is? Pippa asked. About three miles said Marta, good I could do with a bath and a drink of water with ice in it. I'll second that said Marta.

They carried on walking until they came to a clearing in which stood a hospital, that's handy said Pippa. Well, I can at least get a bath in the house I suppose. Well, if the doctors about she will probably let you get a bath, but if it's Matron on her own she is a tyrant. It will be the river, for you.

Marta said laughing. They entered the hospital to find the doctor at the reception desk talking to the receptionist. Hello, Marta what brings you here, we are trying to find Douglas MacDougall, and he's stolen the Jade Healing Mask of the Glummpopo. The Chief is very ill and we don't want to kill him to send him to heaven to get him well. We need the mask, Oh! This is Pippa Plum time traveller, from Celrin in North Wales. Marta said. Hello Pippa call me Gloria said the doctor. Hello, Gloria said Pippa. Would it be possible for me to take a bath, please Pippa asked, it's been nearly seven days since I last took one. We've travelled a long way, if I could have used my wings, it would not have taken us half as long, but in this specialist suit, I forgot about my wings. Next one I won't. Laughed Pippa.

Follow me said Gloria, they walked across the compound, and through the front door of the house,

It's, the third on the left Gloria said. Plenty hot water, no need to skimp, Help yourself to the bubble bath etc.

Oh! Luxury, Pippa said as she sank down into the steaming hot water in the bath, bubbles up to her nose, making her sneeze. She dipped her head into the hot water feeling it relaxing all her muscles, and heaving a sigh of delight, lazed in it. Until there was a sharp knock on the door. Hey, Marta said, have you died in there?

Pippa laughed, No, just enjoying the delights of a steaming hot bath, won't be a minute she said as she climbed out of the bath, wrapped a towel around herself and another round her hair, grabbed her dirty clothes and walked into the spare bedroom to change into her clean clothes.

Mm. That feels good Pippa said. Sorry what did you say Marta asked? Talking to myself said Pippa,

Oh! Go ahead don't mind me Marta said laughing. About half an hour after that Marta immerged looking clean and sparkling for someone who is only two foot something. Are you ready to eat said?

Pippa, the doctor has invited us for dinner. We had that at one o'clock fairy time said Marta.

No, that was lunch Pippa said. Laughing.

Well, whatever you call it I want some laughed Marta.

They took their dirty clothes downstairs with them and put them on the step so they could wash them later. Hi Gloria, finished for the day, No, I'm always on call said Gloria but I can have at least two hours off.

Will a Ham Salad do you with Pineapple Juice to follow asked Gloria? Lovely, both the girls said together, almost as if they were sisters.

Come into the kitchen Gloria said, it's easier to talk to you there. How far do you think Douglas MacDougall will have got Gloria asked? Has he been here? Marta asked. Yes, two days ago, he did not say where he'd been. Did he say where he was headed? Pippa asked. Yes, to Nimbopo Island.

Gloria said. What's on Nimpopo Island Pippa asked? Oh! Did you not know that's where he lives now, bought it a couple of years ago? He got married to a widow from Northumberland. She's really lovely, called Pamella. Oh! You mean Pamela Pippa said, No her proper name is Pamella Jones- Johnson. She was married to a very wealthy man, who died suddenly. It almost killed her. She went into seclusion; they thought that they would never get her back into the life lane again.

Somehow Douglas met her and she began to live again, in his protecting arms as they say. Well, she adores Douglas, they are inseparable. They bought the Island for two point four million, and have lived there ever since. He goes on his trips, sometimes she goes with him sometimes she doesn't.

Well, I have a few words to say to that young man Marta said. I'll fly over after dinner. Want to come with me Pippa? Yes, I'd like to meet this Pamella Jones-Johnson. She sounds like a very nice lady.

You will like her said Gloria. Now eat, please, would you like some black bread? What on earth is black bread Pippa asked? It's made from seaweed and something else Gloria said.

I'll give it a go said Pippa and Marta together, you two sound more like sisters than friends you seem to say everything together. Laughed Gloria.

This Pineapple juice is beautiful Yes, My Girl makes it for me, you have yet to meet my girl Friday I call her. She will be along later, when she's finished work. She my nurse also, we live here together, and share the chores.

Tell me about your trip then Gloria said. Well, I time travelled to get Pippa Plum from Celrin, and we time travelled back to Glummpopo Land. Had a bit of a break and then we travelled to Umboto Land mostly on foot and canoe. Then across the swamp infested with crocodiles, across a quicksand area and then Matumbi's Land where the Gorillas are.

We have to go through the Jungle Maze of the Natouri Tribe yet, before we can go to the Island. That is going to be good fun.

Then we arrived here to your hospital to get a bath and clean up and then asked to this lovely dinner with you.

This black bread is not too bad Pippa said. Would you mind if I have another piece. No help yourself Gloria said.

Well, when dinner was over Pippa said let me do the dishes for you? Marta laughed and said what she means is let the fairy dust do the dishes for you. What's fairy dust asked Gloria? It's a wonderful commodity the fairies have for doing their chores when they have not got time. Oh! What exactly does it do Gloria asked. Well, you sprinkle it on your dishes add some hot water then stand back and wait. Wait for what? Gloria asked. Just watch and see. So as Gloria stood there and watched, the dishes jumped out of the water, dried themselves on the tea towel and flew to the cupboard and put themselves down where they should be. Marvellous, Gloria said where do I get some? Well, I am afraid that you can't get it said Pippa; only fairies can use it I am afraid. Pity I could use some of it in my hospital to do the chores we have not got time to do. Well, Pippa said if I can use your washing machine to clean my clothes, I could use some of my fairy dust to help you in the hospital. Deal said Gloria, come this way, and they walked across the compound to the hospital. Right, we need to clean here, here and here, then there, that, and that. There is also here, here and here and the list was endless, being it was a hospital, but Pippa set too with her water, bucket and fairy dust, mops, clothes and brushes. Then left it to get on with it, while she went to do the washing, she put all the clothes into the washer with some fairy dust and left it to do it job. Next time Gloria went to the hospital she could not believe her eyes. Pippa was just putting all the things away; you mean to say it's only taken you twenty minutes to do this job. Gloria said. No, I have not done the job; the fairy dust did the job. I have been putting washing into the washing machine and now I'm going to put it all away. What! Do you mean Gloria asked, put it away. Well it will be washed, dried, ironed and folded and ready to be put away as the fairy dust does not know yet where you keep everything.

How, What, Why, Gloria could not understand. I told you the fairy dust will do the job; it washes, dries, irons, folded and puts everything where it goes, and when it knows where to go that is.

Oh! Please give me some Gloria said. Please, please, pretty please. Gloria begged and begged.

Sorry, no can do. Pippa said. Gloria was almost in tears, but I want some. Well, you can't have any

Now stop it, please. Pippa said.

Thanks for this Gloria said, you have saved me many hours work. I'm really grateful. No problems Pippa said.

Now I don't know about you, but I am ready for my bed. Pippa said, I'll be up in a minute said Marta.

Goodnight both of you, I'll leave you both to catch up. Thanks again Gloria. Goodnight.

She almost fell up the stairs she was that tired, boy am I ready for my bed. She undressed, cleaned her teeth, gargled and spit out.

Then flew across the landing to her bedroom thinking I haven't used my wings for so long I forgot to fly when I got to the stairs.

She snuggled down after putting the insect net over herself so she would not get bitten in the night, and was soon fast asleep, she did not hear Marta come to bed, or Gloria.

The first thing she heard was the cockerel in the hen house crowing to say Good Morning Day.

Well, Pippa are you ready to tackle the maze today? Well, I suppose we should give it a try.

They were all dressed up in their trekking gear, ready to tackle the maze. They started walking at about nine o'clock fairy time, and by twelve they had arrived at the maze, but decided to have a light meal before tackling the maze. They made sandwiches with some Ham they had got off Gloria, and then they had some fruit. Packed everything up and headed off towards the maze, they had one advantage; in that Marta could fly it was a pity Pippa could not use her wings too. They got into difficulty about half way through, as they kept going back to the same spot, they knew that as they had left little bits of material in the bushes they had passed. I'll fly up and take a look as to which direction we should go, Marta flew up into the air as if it was nothing, took a look around ah! She said that's where we are going wrong. Pippa take a left, left and then right, we kept going left.

Pippa took a left, left and then a right, and took the through exit up to the next level. Marta flew down to join her and then they went left, right, straight, left and right. Now where said Pippa?

I'll fly up and look said Marta. Right sorry I did not mean right, I meant ready. Take a left, straight and right, right, then left. Well, she said we are half way through, now take the straight ahead and then left, then right, right, left, straight, right, left, left, right and so it went on until they were almost out but not quite. Marta flew up and looked oh! Yes, I see we should have gone left but we went right, back up to here Marta said. Then go left and then straight. Ha! Ha! We did it. Good job you could fly Marta. Next time I go on a job

I'm having my wings free. Now we have to get to the Island and that Douglas MacDougall, I'm going to slap his face said Marta, thinking of all the trouble he had caused them. Slap him Pippa shouted I'd like to knock his block off. I'm so mad.

They crossed to the Island in a canoe which was sat there as if waiting for them, Pippa paddled them across to the Island and they beached the canoe. Next they had to walk up what felt like a thousand steps, and they were at his front door. They rang the bell; it played taking a trip down to oh! I can never remember where the trip goes to said Pippa. Well, don't ask me said Marta, door bells are not my forty. Then they were facing Mr Douglas MacDougall. You, low life Marta said I could slap you're Silly face. What have I done to you? Asked Douglas MacDougall, Well, one you stole the Jade Healing Mask which our Chief needs, two we have been through insect infected lands, three we have been through crocodiles infested lands, four we have been through quicksand, five we have been through Gorillas, six we have been through the jungle maze with great difficulty I might add.

Will that do for now. Marta fumed at him. Pippa said I feel like knocking your block off myself, but I am too much of a lady to do it but likewise what she said.

Now hand over the Jade Healing Mask so we can get back to save the Chief's life. Pippa said.

Come in let me get you a drink said Douglas MacDougall.

Pamella Jones-Johnson appeared whatever is the noised about? She asked. These two ladies have come for the Jade Healing Mask of the Glummpopo. What? Why do you think we have it Pamella asked?

One because the coiled snake was left to say it was him who took it. He always left that sign when he took anything Pippa Plum said. Oh! Pamella said, but I should mind my manners ladies said Pamella please come in and take a seat. Let me get you something to drink Lime Juice, No not lime Juice Pippa said we get sqwiffy on that. Pineapple or apple juice would be nice though. I'll have Pineapple Juice if I may said Marta. Thank you.

Here you are Pippa and Marta is it? Yes, they said together. Thank you.

Now, let's discuss the problem, you think we have the Jade Healing Mask am I right? Yes, Pippa said, Douglas left the mark of the coiled snake, like he always does if he takes anything. Well, I am afraid that we have not got it said Douglas and Pamella together. But you must have said Pippa you were in the area. Yes, but we did not take the Jade Healing Mask. We were there on business; we are trying to buy a Gorilla for the Zoo in America. Well, who has taken the mask then? Pippa and Marta were very confused. Only one other person knows of that mask and that is Professor Smithson from the Institute in Western Canada. I bet he got someone to pinch it for him. Try there, would you like another drink? No thank you, we must go, the Chief is very, very ill and if we do not get it back soon he may die.

Pippa you time travel don't you? Said Douglas. Yes, why? Well, that would be the quickest way to go

Then he said. I have no purple fairy dust left here its back at the Glummpopo Village. Well, I can fly you there in my chopper. If you just give me a minute to start her up, thank you, you're very kind.

Pippa said.

Get in but mind your head on the blades, the girls climbed into the helicopter and strapped themselves in. I've never been in a helicopter before said Marta, it's great fun. They were soon back at the Glummpopo Village where Pippa picked up another supply of fairy dust. Now, what said Marta.

Well, I make a circle in the ground and add the fairy dust to make a circle, then I hold your hand tightly, say the magic words lfewgergeoirhgeproijhepoh Institute WesternCanada.

The wind started to blow and it blew until it became a whirlwind, then it turned into a full blown tornado sucking them up and spinning, spinning until it was in Western Canada, where it dropped them outside the institute and soon the wind died down and it was all calm again.

Well, now lets find that low life Pippa said.

Proffessor Smithson please they asked the receptionist, room 435 2nd floor said the receptionist would you like me to tell him you're coming, no thank you we want to surprise him. Boy, will he get a surprise said Pippa.

Here it is, 435 Professor Smithson. They knocked and entered without waiting for a reply.

How may I help you ladies the smarmy Professor said.? You may help us by giving us the Jade Healing Mask you took from the Glummpopo. Pippa said.

Never heard of it said the Professor. Wait a minute said Marta? She said some magic words jgeojy3oyj3ojyohjhojohy Suddenly, there was a whoosing noise, then a knocking noise as though something was trying to get through something, a door perhaps said Pippa. They searched all over for the door but could find nothing. Still the noise persisted, knocking and banging, rattling, shaking.

It sounds like its coming through the wall, said Pippa. There must be a secret door or something,

They felt all around for anything, bookcases, tables, cupboards suddenly smash! It came through

The wall, the Jade Healing Mask of the Glummpopo was restored to its owner well one of them at least. Marta slapped the Professor hard across his face. You're a mean man taking this from poor people, why? I wanted to test it for its magical powers said the Professor. All you had to do was come and ask, and as long as you did it in the village you could have done your research there.

What about it then said the Professor? Too late now, said Marta if our Chief dies because of this you will be cursed forever. That is no idle threat she said, this mask will have cursed you, we don't need to do anything said Marta, and if you start feeling funny then you're in trouble. No one can help you, ever.

Good bye Professor, good luck, you will need it.

Pippa and Marta carrying the Jade Mask, stood in the circle. Purple fairy dust, magic words, noihgjkb neoi4th39q8h3g, the wind turning, spinning, spinning, whirlwind turning into a tornado scooping them up and placing them down in the Glummpopo Village. All safe and sound. They rushed to the Chiefs hut. How is he they asked? Nearly gone I am afraid they said, they knelt down beside him and placed the Jade Mask on his face. Suddenly, it started to glow and the diamonds started to shine, and then all of a sudden the Chief spoke in a very low voice. My people I am well, again. Place me on my throne that I might see you all again. So they lifted him up and placed him on his throne and he looked around at his people and smiled, I am home, amongst my people. Let's say a prayer to the Great God of the Heavens and thank him for his protection. Which they did, and they sang and they chanted, chanted and they sang. Everything was right with their world and their people, and their Chief. They laughed and sang and where happy, for the Jade Healing Mask was returned to them,

They were whole again, the sun was shining, the sky was blue, and the little birds sang.

PIPPA PLUM TIME TRAVELLER

No.
3

Pippa Plum was doing her garden at her new cottage; it was called Poppy Field Cottage. It was named that as it was beside a field of Poppies that grew there every year. She thought at the age of thirty fairy years it was time to find somewhere other than her mother's house to live. So she looked around the little village of Celrin where she was born and went to school and lived. It was a lovely little village of fairies, but they were getting new people all the time, they had a little man with dark skin who was an African Medicine Man a very knowledgeable man who could do all sorts of wonderful things with his magic. He made potions that if someone had a bad leg he could make a medicine or cream and within a couple of days it was healed. He could bring a time traveller into the village from Africa a little man who had a bone through his nose and was only two foot high but very knowledgeable too. He wore a grass skirt and had gold bands around his arms and gold jewellery around his neck which he had made from gold he had found near where he lived. The village he lived in had become very rich as he also found diamonds there, so the Little Man helped them all. So it was a very good life they all had, no one was hungry, or cold, or ill as the little man time travelled to meet an African Medicine Man who now lived in the village of Celrin and all he had to do was tell him what was wrong with the person and he could heal them from Celrin and send them medicine back with the little man.

So when she found Poppy Field Cottage beside a river on one side and a poppy field on the other a river. She fell in love with it I must buy it thought Pippa Plum it would be ideal for me. She could use the water from the river for her garden. She could fish for trout; she could dangle her feet in the water if she wanted too, when it was all hers of course. So she flew straight to the person who was selling the cottage and asked them could she buy it and how much was it, when could she move in, all these questions running through her head at the same time. Well, the owner said she could move in any time she wished as long as she could afford it. The paper was signed and they shook hands in agreement. Pippa was thrilled and flew home to her mother's to tell her that she had bought herself a cottage. Where her mother said? It's by the river at the side is a Field of Poppies and it's called Poppy Field Cottage. Oh! Yes her mother said I know it, who is the owner I have been sworn to secrecy about that said Pippa. Strange said her mother to Pippa, yes, very said Pippa, but that is how it must be. When are you moving in then said her mother? Oh! Soon, but I must pack everything up first. I also need to clean the cottage first. Would you like some help with that said her mother, if you have time, perhaps, tomorrow? I am free tomorrow said her mother, what time would be suitable?

Oh! Perhaps around one o'clock. Fine, I'll meet you there then said her Mother. Mum what's the matter you seem a bit off? I am not feeling too well this morning said her mother I have not been sleeping too well lately. Why? What's been the problem? Oh! I worry about your father that's all

He is not too well, but I don't know what's up with him, he won't tell me. I will see what I can do Pippa said. When is Papa home? He will be back around two o'clock to-day. I will see him then and ask what's wrong, if I can find out what's wrong my friend Mr Mawumba the African Medicine Man

Friend of mine will help he's very good, he can heal from afar. He can make legs heal in two days, he has powers we still don't know of, and he is truly amazing. Don't worry Mother, I'll help somehow.

Now, I must get on, will you be alright? Yes dear, now I will her mother said to Pippa.

Pippa flew upstairs to get her bag, I'm off to the bank now, to sort out my finances and pay for the cottage. See you later, Mother. Is there anything you need from the Village? No, dear I'm fine.

Pippa flew out of the door and away through the fields and into the village. Hello Mr Golightly, nice day today she said, as she walked into the bank. Yes, dear Mr Golightly said. He put a bag of cash in through the tillers window, may I pay that in Margaret please. Yes, Mr Golightly, current account or shop accounts? Shop please. Mr Golightly answered. Here is your receipt Mr Golightly Margaret said.

Thank you Margaret, see you again. Bye Mr Golightly.

Now Miss Plum How can I help you? I wish to see Mr Howarth please. I have found a cottage to live in, and wish to buy it. Oh! That's lovely said Margaret; I will ask Mr Howarth if he's free. Could you wait a moment said Margaret. Yes, said Pippa.

Miss Plum would you like to come this way, Mr Howarth is free now. Pippa followed her into Mr Howarth's office. Welcome Pippa said Mr Howarth, glad to hear your news. How can I help you?

Well, I need to pay for the cottage so I want to sell some of the shares my Nanna left me, if that is possible. Yes, of course it is. How much will you need? Well, the cottage is three hundred and forty fairy coins. So as long as I have that it will be fine. I can keep the rest in my trust fund till I need it

If that's alright. Pippa said. Fine Mr Howarth said. Then who shall I make the cheque out too? I am afraid I cannot tell you that, I must have it in fairy gold coins because that is how my seller wants it, and they are going abroad and need the cash. No banks where they will be living you see Pippa said.

Thank you and good day Mr Howarth. Bye Pippa, how is your father keeping? I don't know Mr Howarth mums really worried about him; do you know anything about his illness? He told me in confidence Pippa; you will have to ask him yourself. Thank you Mr Howarth I will now I know something's wrong.

Pippa went to the fashion designer who made her time travelling suit and asked if she could make another but for it to allow for her to use her wings. That won't be too difficult Pippa, she said.

When will you want it for? The sooner the better please, I never know when I am going anywhere.

Pippa said. Right I will get right onto it, then. Same colour pink, how about purple, not my colour said Pippa I much prefer, pink. O.k. said her fashion designer said Pink it is.

Bye then call me when it's ready please. Will do was the reply.

Now, what's next Oh! Yes, toothpaste then it's back to talk to Papa.

Pippa went to get the toothpaste from the local shop, had a chat to the greengrocer and said could he deliver some fruit to his mother she was looking a bit peaky, a lovely basket mind, not a bag or box but a lovely big basket.

Thank you said the greengrocer; I will get right on to it. Bye Pippa.

Bye Pippa said. It's funny she thought I can never remember his name? I must look next time I go there.

Pippa made for home and a chat with her Papa. Hi! Mother, I'm home are you alright. Yes, dear I am just having a lie down called her mother; I have a bit of a headache, that's all.

Papa will soon be home shall I send him up? No dear it's o.k. I won't be long, just need to clear this headache.

Would you like a cuppa, Oh! That would be nice, dear she called. Be right up, with it.

Pippa flew into the kitchen, popped some fairy dust into a cup added the fairy tea and waited, put in a little honey and flew upstairs to give it to her mother. Thank you dear, her Mother said. Need anything else. No dear I'm fine. I'll leave you then said Pippa.

Hello, anyone home called a voice, hello I'm just coming said Pippa.

Here is the basket of fruit for your Mother dear said the greengrocer, gosh! That was quick said Pippa, how much do I owe you, five fairy coins said the greengrocer. Here you are that's right I think Pippa said.

Thank you Pippa said the greengrocer. Say hello to your Mother for me.

I will do that, she has a headache and is having a lie down Pippa said.

Hello, Mr Green how are you said Pippa's Papa. I am fine Mr Plum said Mr Green how's the family?

Blooming said Mr Green, well I must be off. Bye all called Mr Green.

Pippa flew over and kissed her Papa, You know Papa, I could never remember his name, whose name Mr Green isn't that funny when he a Greengrocer. You'd think I'd remember. Her Papa just laughed. How are you today Papa she said? I am fine dear why? No you're not said Pippa, I asked Mr Howarth and he said I had to ask you. Well, all right I'm not it's just a slight heart murmur the doctor

Said nothing to worry about just to take things easy. That's why I am coming home at two now, instead of five thirty. Can I get you anything asked Pippa, some fairy tea would be nice dear, where's your Mother. Having a lie down she's got a bad head again, I'm getting very worried about her headaches, she's having too many. I will ask Mr Mawumba for some help he's a great doctor, you know he can heal from afar and if you have a bad knee, leg arm whatever he can make it better in two days, yes, just two days. I am going over after to see him; I'll ask him to say a little prayer for you too, is that alright. Fine her Papa said. I am going up to see your mother would you mind bringing me my tea upstairs, no Papa that's o.k. What flavour so you want? Raspberry thanks.

Hello my love, how are you today? I have one of my screaming headaches; again, it's almost gone now. Oh! And I was just coming up to join you he laughed. That's fine dear I don't mind. Ah! Pippa with my tea, thank you darling, that's lovely.

Pippa flew into her room, and started to collect a few of her things together, ready to pack them up.

Boxes, I need boxes, she flew in to ask her Papa, have we any cardboard boxes in the attic, yes, dear you just have to make them up, they are folded flat her Papa said.

Pippa flew into the attic, ah! There you are? She said to the boxes. Oh! What's this, she saw something on the floor, and it looks like a diamond she said. When she picked it up and looked at it,

Tried to cut the mirror it marked it, so you are a diamond she said. She flew downstairs with the boxes and put them in her room, then flew into her parent's room where they were resting and showed her Papa what she had found. Well, well, where did you find this dear her Papa said. On the floor in the attic, why did you lose it? No dear your mother did about thirty years ago, he said and laughed, the one place we did not look was the attic. Well, I will get it set in another ring for our next anniversary, she will be so pleased she had not lost it altogether, Said her Papa. Thank you darling, I'll show her when she awakes. She finally got off to sleep. I am going to have forty winks too if that's alright he said. Call me when dinner is ready he said. Yes, Papa.

Pippa started to pack the boxes, It's funny I never thought I had so much stuff, I seem to have been packing for two years. Then she thought well, I probably have as I keep getting called away to solve problems. This should be the last though, I have nearly finished, and the cottage will look lovely by the time I get everything in it. Then she flew downstairs to get the dinner going, she was going to do Pasta tonight they had not had it for a while. She sliced the onions up small, and fried them in butter until they were tender, added the garlic, bacon pieces, tomato puree and some herbs, and cooked it then she put in some chopped tomatoes from a tin believe it or not, they make much better pasta than fresh ones. When that was ready, she boiled some water added some salt, and put in the pasta cooked till it was aldante, drained it and added butter. Put it in a big dish, added the sauce and put it to keep warm in the oven while she called her parents, she flew upstairs and called Mother, Papa dinner is ready. Yes dear they called be right down.

By the time they got down Pippa had set the table and placed the meal on the little box with a light under it. Oh! Pippa this does look nice, her parents said. She had grated some cheese to put on the top. Oh! this tastes lovely wherever did you get the receipe, Well, I have two little fairy friends Celine the Cygnet fairy and Catrin the Clover Fairy and their Nanna Pam gave me the receipe, she had it from her Italian Aunty, who used to look after her In her school holidays. She has quite a few receipe's she has passed on. She has a fabulous receipe for Oat Cookies; I must make you some next time I come. Do you realise it's almost two years that I have been trying to move out of here, because I kept getting called away. Pippa said. Her Mother and Papa laughed we wondered how long it would take you to notice, they said. Not that we mind, of course.

Well, I'm off to the cottage now with the rest of my stuff, please come to tea tomorrow; I'd love to have you there. What time asked her Mother about five thirty if that's alright.

See you then said her parents together. Bye then.

Pippa got her little pony Sunbeam out and put his cart on to his harness and put all her things into the cart, and away they flew down to Poppy Field Cottage. Hello, little cottage, you are finally mine,

She said, as she placed the last box inside the door, put sunbeam in his field and the cart in the barn.

She lit a fire and sat in front of it, she was just nodding off when her phone went. Could I speak to Miss Pippa Plum said the voice of Officialdom. Speaking said Pippa, Miss Plum this is the Government of Arubiastan, we have lost one of our most treasured possessions and wonder if you could help we find it. When would you want me there? A.S.A.P. Well, I am just in the middle of moving she said would tomorrow be all right. Fine said the voice of Officialdom. By the way, money no object it said, Fine said Pippa she you soon. Well, little cottage, here we go again, if I ever get to move in here to live it will take a miracle thought Pippa. Well, I suppose I had better get to bed.

She flew upstairs got her pyjamas on and flew into the bathroom to brush her teeth. Flee into bed and settled down for the night, snuggling up in a ball, until morning.

Her fairy alarm awoke her at five thirty a.m. Well, I must get up and sort things out she thought to herself.

She went into the bathroom, washed and brushed her teeth, got dressed and made herself breakfast. Put her fairy dust into the sink added water and left it to do its job.

Then she packed her backpack with her usual essentials, she was just about to go when the phone rang, hello Pippa your new time travel suit is ready, oh! Wonderful she said to her fashion designer just in time I am off on my travels again. Well, call in and collect it then, you may as well wear it as it will enable you to fly. 'Matild' said.

Be there as soon as possible she said. Oh! Absolutely wonderful she said to herself, just what I needed.

She looked around her little cottage, goodbye little cottage see you soon, She closed and locked the door as she did not know when she would get back, Oh! Crumbs she thought Mum and dad? I must tell them, I'll call on the way over, she flew to her parents' house and told her parents what was happening, could they keep an eye on sunbeam. Then I really must dash still have to call to pick up my new suit. See you when I get home, love you both. Bye and she was gone.

Hello anyone about she called to her friend the fashion designer 'Matild' hello Pippa I'm up here in the attic, be right there. Your suit is hung up in the dressing room for you. Pippa flew to the dressing room and looked Oh! 'Matild' you've done it again, thought Pippa. It was brilliant, as usual, similar to her other suit but the helmet was different and she could have her wings free, she put it on. Oh!

Wonderful, it's so light even lighter than her other suit, although that folded up into almost nothing.

Great, I may as well keep it on. Must dash 'Matild' sorry, Bye called 'Matild'. You look great in it.

Pippa flew to the oak woods where she knew there was plenty of room, to make the circle.

She drew a circle on the ground, placed some fairy dust in and around the circle, stood in the middle, with her backpack on, and waited. Suddenly, it started the wind, stronger, stronger until it was a whirlwind spinning, spinning, turning; turning tornado sucked her up as she said the magic words Nvweinspn bmQIWURF iroehnba'ws. Arubiastan, then before she knew it she was there outside the Embassy, She got herself composed and walked up to the guard outside, hello My name is Pippa Plum I have come to see the Governor. This way Miss we have been waiting for you. He took her into the embassy and up some steps; this is Miss Plum to see the Governor. Right Miss Plum follow me said the Official voice that rang her. Welcome, welcome Miss Plum I have so been looking forward to seeing you said the Governor would you like some tea? I have brought my fairy tea she said, I was not sure if you had any or not. Yes, we knew you had special tea and so we got some in. Raspberry or Strawberry, Blackcurrant and he went through his list. Pippa laughed Raspberry will do thank you, said Pippa. The tea soon arrived and Pippa sipped it slowly, thinking what on earth do they want me to find?

The Governor started to speak, well Pippa he said the reason I have asked you here is one of ships has been stolen and it was carrying a load of gold and silver ingots worth about seventy billion in your currency. Wow, Pippa said. Yes, said the Governor, we want you to find it for us. We have a rough calculation of where it disappeared; it's between the Bermuda Triangle and its surrounding area. I have the co-ordinates for you; everything you need to know is on this laptop. Thank you said Pippa. I will look at it later, but does this mean that I will have to dive to the bottom of the sea to look for it.

Oh! No said the Governor, it has not been sunk, but where ever it is, it's on the sea or land.

The distress signal was sent out and we got the co-ordinates from the signal, but where it is now, we don't know as the signal has stopped sending or it is being prevented from sending the signal, there is an on/off switch, the governor said.

Thank you governor, I will go and do my searches and look at the laptop, luckily for me I am a fairy and we have lots of special powers to help us find things, and then Pippa left the governor's Office.

She went to her room that the embassy had given her, to look at all the information that was in the laptop and other paperwork. Mm. She said to herself, the Bermuda triangle could be the problem it can send all the dials on the instruments haywire. I wonder! She picked up the phone after sprinkling it with fairy dust; it changed her voice to that of the governor. Hello, this is the Governor of Aurubiastan speaking could you please give me the tides, winds, weather reports for the 22nd of May, for around the Bermuda Triangle please I am on extension 55 at the Embassy today. Phone me there, thank you, and bye.

She went back to looking at the information, thinking about things, Latitude...........North, Longitude...........West, Mm. I wonder, she got out her purple fairy dust and sprinkled some on the map, just where the ship vanished. It showed that the ship went here she said, but the distress signal was sent from there. Mm very unusual, why was it such a distance from the other map reference?

She put the fairy dust from the map back in its bag, sprinkled it over the other area she was thinking of. Ah! That's strange too. Wow, could that be where it is. Just then the phone rang the answer to her questions about wind, weather etc. Is that Pippa Plums Office asked the voice? Yes, it is, can I help you? Yes, could I speak to the Governor please, Yes, just one moment Please, she turned as if talking to someone, he'll be there in a minute said Pippa. She sprinkled the fairy dust onto the phone again, hello, this is the Governor speaking. Yes, thank you

Well, that helps a little, thought Pippa. She sprinkled the fairy dust over the paper information she had, it showed something very unusual occurred in the Bermuda Triangle at that time. What could it be she thought to herself? Boy, I need some fairy tea, she rang the receptionist, Please said Pippa may I have some fairy tea please, Strawberry, thank you.

A knock came on the door, tea for Pippa Plum the boy called, thank you do come in. A little elf appeared carrying the tray. Oh! Hello, she said I did not know Elves work with humans, I'm doing a research trip said the Elf I'm in disguise. Pippa laughed, but I can see your ears, she said. That's o.k. I said it was a genetic problem and no one has bothered me since, he laughed, well must g, if you need anything else please call. My name is Hubert by the way. Bye Hubert, Pippa said. Oh! Is there anything I can help you with in that he said eyeing up the paperwork, well perhaps you could. When do you finish work? Pippa said. At two thirty said Hubert? Right meet I here then Pippa said.

Hubert left the office smiling, boy this could be fun, it will make a pleasant change from taking the post and trays of tea or coffee everywhere.

This tea is very good thought Pippa, I wonder if they make it different to me, must ask Hubert.

She picked up the paperwork and poured the fairy dust back into the bag, I wonder if I could time travel to Bermuda tonight, must check on the winds etc., I suppose Hubert could come with me, if he's not busy. She sipped her tea, must phone Mother and Papa to see how they are. She rang the receptionist; do you think it will be alright for me to phone home? I'll check first Miss Plum.

As she turned to walk away from the phone, it rang. Hello, said Pippa. Miss Plum you may phone home, but you will have to put 01 in front of the number. Thank you said Pippa and she put down the phone.

Now, what she thought, I suppose I could fly so far, no I'll use the fairy dust and time travel, yes, tonight will have to be the time around five- five thirty, sorted. Pippa said.

She finished her tea and she'd eaten her cake, ah! Well back to work. Knuckle down Pippa come on.

She opened the laptop, and switched it on, pressed the document section and waited for it to come up with document, she pressed the open button and the file opened for her to read it. That's very interesting she said. She wrote it down on the paperwork, just to keep it fresh in her head.

Longitude......... South and Latitude East........ Mm I see Pippa said. Well, now with the Longitude........ North and the Latitude............ West. That's a distance of thirty miles, Could a ship travel that distance in the space of thirteen minutes. I don't think so, but I will have to check at the Admiralty later. Now, I'm off to lunch. She wrote a note in case anyone needed her and left it stuck to the door. Flew down the stairs and out through the front door, to a little café' across the road.

Hello, Pippa what can I get you said the waiter, coffee and a chicken sandwich, Pippa said, thanks.

He came back with a tray, Coffee, sugar, cream or milk. One chicken sandwich on rye bread you have don't you, he asked? Yes, that's fine Pippa said. Thank you.

Whilst she was sat eating her sandwich she kept thinking about the puzzle of where the ship was,

It has to be somewhere, but where? Longitude........North Latitude..... West, Longitude ....South Latitude........East thirty miles difference in 13 minutes. 13 into 30 is 2 with 4 over, no still I can't figure it out. 30 miles in any direction? Bermuda Triangle. Gauges altered. Magnetic North.

Latitude........ North Longitude........West Latitude......... South Longitude..........East Latitude......... East Longitude..... North Latitude............West Longitude.........South. Mm

That does not make sense either.

Latitude North East, Longitude South West.

Latitude South East, Longitude North West. Mm possibly? One or the other of these, it makes more sense this way. I will have to time travel back to when the ship was in the Bermuda Triangle and get on board, use my invisibility cape, and just watch. Yes, that's possibly the right idea. Tonight, I will ask Hubert to come. Oh! He should be here by now he said two thirty. It was three thirty before Hubert could get away. Knock, knock enter called Pippa. Hi Hubert said. Sorry I'm late but they kept me at work, someone became sick and had to go home. That's all right Pippa said, I'm going tonight around five thirty. I am going to time travel back to when the ship was in the Bermuda Triangle use my invisibility cape and hide and board and see what happens Pippa said. Won't that be dangerous for you? No I have special powers so they won't find me even without my invisibility cape. What about me, well you can come if you want to, but I have not got another suit like mine. Pippa said.

Oh! I have something similar at home and an invisibility cape too. So that won't be a problem said Hubert. Fine then meet me back here at five thirty. Pippa said. I'm going to dinner now see you later.

Bye said Hubert, see you later.

Pippa flew down the stairs and across the hall to the swinging doors, and walked through hailed a taxi and said the Belmont Hotel please. Yes, Miss Plum said the taxi driver, how do you know my name said Pippa. Oh! We've all been given your photo and have to help anyway we can the Governors Orders, you do not need to pay us either, that has been taken care off. That's just great said Pippa, and she sat back and enjoyed her ride. A few minutes later she arrived at the Belmont Hotel. Went up to get changed, and go down to dinner. She stood and waited for the Concierge to come to ask her how many dining? Just one please she said.' Would you like a seat by the window perhaps so you can look out and see the view? Yes, that would be lovely said Pippa. He held the chair out for her to sit down and then gave her the menu. I will come back in a while he said. Thank you said Pippa.

As she sat and looked at the menu, she had a quick glance around, not many in here tonight she thought. The concierge' came back, has mademoiselle seen what she would like to eat and drink, yes please I will have the chicken with potatoes dauphine, petite poi, carrots with stuffing and gravy,

Followed by Chocolate Éclair's and fruit, and to drink I'd like an Orange and Pineapple drink, thank you, Peter.

It will take a little while said Peter, would you like your Orange and Pineapple Juice while you wait.

Yes, please. Pippa said.

Peter came back carrying her juice, will you need anything else Miss Plum. How did you know my name? Pippa asked. Don't tell me the Governor sent you my photo, yes, miss how did you guess?

The taxi driver said the same, she laughed. Dinner is on the house miss; don't tell me the governor, Yes Miss. Peter said.

Ah! Here is your dinner, enjoy. Thank you, Peter. Pippa said.

Pippa sat eating her dinner and as she ate she thought, the puzzle was not yet solved, but the end was in sight.

Did you enjoy your chicken mademoiselle Peter asked? Yes thank you Peter Pippa said.

Now for the treat said Peter, Chocolate Éclair's, followed by fresh fruit basket. Enjoy?

Pippa took one look at the Éclair's Oh! Scrummy thought Pippa. Then she had some grapes, a peach, and two Apricots. Well, that's me beaten; I'm full to the brim.

Well, that was glorious, Pippa said but I must away, back to my job. Thank you Peter and would you say thank you to the staff too. Pippa asked.

Yes, mademoiselle Peter said. Bye.

Pippa flew to the Office at the embassy, to meet Hubert. It was almost five thirty, so he should not be too long. I will change into my suit and sort out my invisibility cape. Then we needn't stop anywhere. Purple fairy dust in pockets, instruments yes, that's it, right I am ready to go. Now all I need is Hubert.

Knock, knock enter called Pippa, Hello, Pippa here I am, already suited and invisibility cape at the ready. Hubert said.

Let's go then, Pippa said. I'm glad you have wings; we need to fly a little way out of town.

When they reached the outskirts of the town, they checked around to make sure no one was about.

Pippa drew a circle in the dirt, sprinkled fairy dust into the circle she had just made. She took hold of Hubert's hands and said hold on tight. Suddenly, a purple cloud started swirling around them, turning, turning, spinning, spinning, Whirlwind, spinning, turning until it became a tornado, scooped them up into the centre and as Pippa said the few magic words ncv'woijgbna8itg]wne'rnbe'

Latitude North by North West, Longitude South by South East. Then next they were stood in the middle of the ship in their invisibility capes, in the Bermuda Triangle. It was almost the time that the ship disappeared.

Five more minutes she whispered to Hubert, suddenly, they were moving not by sea, not by land but by air, like a big magnet had scooped them up. Thirteen minutes later, they were where??????

Oh! My goodness Pippa said, Look where we are????? Where???????? Hubert said. We are in a ship yard and it looks like the ship is being made into another ship, they are adding things and taking things off, changing the name to Admiral Nelson of London. We have found the ship, no Bermuda Triangle force, No attack just a great, great big Magnet, on two helicopters.

Now, back to base, Pippa said, but keep your invisibility cape on, until we are well out of sight.

Wilko, Hubert said. Whose Wilko said Pippa, just a joke; they say it on the television when the spy's are working with walkie talkies. They say Wilko over and out. Honestly Hubert I give up. Pippa said.

Well, thank you for your help Hubert, off home now. See you tomorrow. Bye Pippa. Hubert said.

Pippa took off her pink suit and folded it up nicely and put it in her backpack. Left the office and flew down to pick up the taxi to her Hotel. HI, Pippa the taxi driver called, want a lift to the Hotel.

Yes, please Pippa said and sat back to enjoy the ride.

Pippa called the taxi driver, wake up you're here. Um, Murmured Pippa, Wake up Pippa you're at the Hotel. Oh! Sorry, thank you. Bit of a hectic day.

She walked into the hotel; her wings were still hurting with all the flying. It's funny how you take things for granted said Pippa to herself. She took the lift up to her room, opened the door and flopped on the bed in exhaustion. She was so tired she could not even undress but fell asleep and did not wake up until nine the next day. She only woke because the phone rang.

Um, Hello Pippa said, Oh! Sorry mademoiselle the Governor is on the phone for you, yes, thank you please put him on. Hello Governor have I got some good news for you Pippa said. I will be there in half an hour. Thank you said the governor. See you then.

Pippa flew into the bathroom had a quick shower, brushed her teeth, and dressed.

Flew downstairs, through the door and hailed a taxi, Hello Pippa get in.

Thank you Henry, Pippa said. Here you are safe and sound said Henry. Say hello to the governor for me. Yes, I will Henry. Thank you Pippa said.

Pippa flew up, up, up the stairs, to her little office, collected her things to show the governor. Knocked on his door, enter called the governor. Pippa entered the room well; your ship did not go by land or sea governor but by air. What do you mean Pippa? The Governor asked.

Well, you know I have special powers and things to help me. Pippa said. Yes, the governor said, although I am not sure what they are. Well, I have a special suit that protects me, and an invisibility cape, fairy dust, and a special elf friend. Pippa laughed. Well, Pippa said we time travelled back into the past and landed on the ship before it disappeared and waited when all of a sudden there was this loud bang, bang and we were suddenly airborne. Two giant magnets one each end of the ship and up it went. Where did you say it was? The Governor said. Well, it was in a dockyard called 'We take your wreck and make it better.' They took things off the ship, put things on it and altered the name to Admiral Nelson of London. Where it is now, you can find out by placing this gadget on your computer map. Thank you Pippa, The Government of Aurubiastan is very pleased with your work. There will be a celebration dinner tonight where his Majesty will present you with the star of Aurubiastan. Hope you can make it Pippa said the governor. Yes, I can thank you Pippa said.

What time? Asked Pippa. On or around seven the governor said I will send a car for you.

Thank you said Pippa See you there then.

She took a taxi to the Hotel and flew to the bathroom, took a shower and washed her hair.

Got out her little black dress and jewellery, Put her hair up into a coil, a little lip gloss on.

Now, I am ready, for anything. She walked gracefully down the stairs, holding her head high.

Car for Miss Pippa Plum called the boy. Car for Miss Pippa Plum, here I am Pippa called.

This way Miss Plum said the boy. Pippa followed him, to the waiting car where he opened the door for her. She got into the car and he closed the door. The car was driven by a man dressed in Uniform of what she could not see. They arrived at the Governors Mansion and she was helped out by this gorgeous hunk in a Navy Uniform. This was Miss Plum, said the Navy man my name is Geoffrey Elliott. Mademoiselle. He said with a French accent, Hello Geoffrey she said my name is Pippa. Yes, I know he said. I have been asked to escort you to the dinner; the governor is my Uncle on my Mother's side.

The ladies maid took her coat and placed it on the rack with a little label saying Pippa Plum.

Care for a drink Pippa, Geoffrey asked, yes, please Orange and Pineapple Juice. He walked towards the bar and asked for the Orange and Pineapple Juice and a' Mitie' for himself. Then took them back to their table and sat down. What have you been up to lately Pippa asked Geoffrey? Well, I time travel to help people out said Pippa. How do you time travel then? Well, you know I am a fairy and that gives me special powers. I could take you sometime but you would have to swear an oath on pain of death not to tell anyone the secrets you see. That would be fun sometime when I am not too busy. So why did you come to Arubiastan? Well, I came to find the ship that disappeared, your Uncle asked me to find it, which I did. I am collecting my star tonight. Pippa said. Oh! I say, well done. Geoffrey said. Thanks Pippa said. How about a dance? Love to. Do you come here often, No Pippa said actually, it's the first time I've been here, nice place though I'll come again.

Well, ladies and gentlemen please take your seats for the dinner, said the governor. Pippa and Geoffrey you're next to me called the governor. Pippa walked round the table to her seat and the governor held her seat for her. Thank you kind sir, Pippa said.

Well, there was a seven course meal, followed by fruit and cheese. Wow, Pippa said I am what you might call full to the brim, lovely. Another drink mademoiselle Peter asked. Yes, Orange and Pineapple please. Pippa said.

Ladies and Gentlemen said the Governor, please welcome his Royal Highness Prince Adam, everyone started to clap. Will Miss Pippa Plum please step onto the stage please asked the governor?

Pippa walked up to the stage and up some steps onto it. Your Majesty may I introduce Miss Pippa Plum. Pippa this is his Majesty Prince Adam. Pippa on behalf of my country I wish to show both mine and my countries gratitude for your service to us both. You found our missing vessel plus all the ingots of silver and gold. May I please present you with the Star of Arubiastan with our thanks? Prince Adam said. Thank you you're majesty, I am highly honoured. Everyone stood up and cheered, and clapped and cheered they were so delighted about Pippa helping their country.

By the time Pippa had come down off cloud nine they had cleared away the tables and chairs and everything was set up for dancing. The band was playing a waltz, Geoffrey asked her to dance and he led her onto the floor, and they started to dance and she felt as light as a feather. It was like she was flying and then she suddenly realized that, that was what she was doing, Oh! Sorry Geoffrey I got carried away. Um, said Geoff what? Oh! He had not noticed she had been flying he had, had his eyes shut while they were dancing. Sorry, said Geoffrey I need a rest, my feet are killing me. Trust me to put new shoes on, before a dance. He laughed.

Say when you are ready to go home, said Geoffrey. In about another half an hour will be fine said Pippa.

They sat and talked for a while, Geoffrey introduced her to some more people she did not know, and then they left together. He drove her home and said goodnight. When do you go home Pippa well, sometime today she said. Pity I am not due to go back to sea until tomorrow. Geoffrey said.

Well, I could stay another day if you'd like Pippa said. That would be really nice Geoffrey said.

I'd like that. All right I'll stay until tomorrow night, but I cannot stay any later, my father is ill and mums not too well either, so I need to check on them. I'm not usually away this long. Being a time-traveller seems to be taking me away a lot longer every time I go anywhere.

Here you are my lady, back at your hotel all safe and sound. Geoffrey said. Night Pippa said and thank you and kissed Geoffrey on his cheek to say thank you. See you tomorrow.

She watched him walk away, into the night and as she walked into the hotel took the lift and walked into her room. Threw her coat on the bed and undressed, flew into the bathroom washed her face and brushed her teeth. Flew to the bed, snuggled down into it and fell fast asleep, did not waken until late morning, gosh! Why do I feel so tired, I just feel so exhausted lately, gosh! I must go to see a doctor when I get back. I must be sickening for something.

The phone rang she walked slowly, to pick it up and said hello, Pippa is that you? Yes, it's me she said Hi this is Geoffrey would you like to go sailing? Yes, please Pippa said. When? In about thirty minutes he said. I'll be in the lobby.

She sat in the lobby waiting for Geoffrey, reading a book whilst she waited for him, suddenly; he was there in front of her, holding some roses. Hi, he said. Hi she said, smiling at him. Are you ready, he said? Yes, when you are she said. They left the hotel holding hands, walking towards his car.

He held the door open for her and she climbed in. They drove off into the sun, to enjoy the day together.

Pippa came back to her hotel to pack up her things, and return to her time in Celrin. She took a taxi to the edge of town where she asked him to drop her, but miss there is nothing here. That's fine she said I'd like to sit and have some time to enjoy the countryside. All right if you're sure. Gerald said.

Thank you Gerald said Pippa nice to have met you.

Pippa drew a circle In the earth, poured the purple fairy dust into the groove, stood in the centre and waited for the purple cloud to appear, then it started, turning, turning, spinning, spinning whirlwind, turning, spinning until it turned into a tornado and scooped her up, into the air, all the time turning and spinning, she spoke the magic wordsnkipgojewhKGTGNDmkffmkjgkg HOME CELRIN. HOME CELRIN and before she knew it she was home in Celrin almost at her own front door,

She smiled and said hello little cottage, she turned the key in the door, said hello sitting room I'm home, no more trips till I sort myself out. I'm just so tired lately, and that's not right.

She picked up the phone and called her parents, Hello Mother I'm back, is Papa all right yes, dear he is fine and so am I nice to know your home, and will you be over for tea later. Will tomorrow do I am bushed; I'm just going to have a cup of fairy tea and go to bed. Fine see you around five darling, good night and god bless. Night Mother, give my love to Papa. I love you both very much.

She flew upstairs, put on her pyjamas as it was a little bit chilly, brushed her teeth and snuggled up in her bed and slept until she awoke, when she awoke, it was almost three in the afternoon. She just lay there, in the stillness and listened. Just feeling utterly, worn out. She got up around four thirty and washed and dressed, did her hair and sat and waited until it was time to go to see her parents for tea. Then she got sunbeam from the field, put her saddle on, and galloped over to her parents' house for tea.

We will leave Pippa there with her parents, but she has many more adventures.